To Sczerina Perot, the greatest helper I know
—E. S. P.

STERLING CHILDREN'S BOOKS
New York

An Imprint of Sterling Publishing Co., Inc.
122 Fifth Avenue
New York, NY 10011

ISBN 978-1-4549-4088-3

Distributed in Canada by Sterling Publishing Co., Inc.
c/o Canadian Manda Group, 664 Annette Street
Toronto, Ontario M6S 2C8, Canada
Distributed in the United Kingdom by GMC Distribution Services
Castle Place, 166 High Street, Lewes, East Sussex BN7 1XU, England
Distributed in Australia by NewSouth Books
University of New South Wales, Sydney, NSW 2052, Australia

For information about custom editions, special sales, and premium and corporate purchases,
please contact Sterling Special Sales at 800-805-5489 or specialsales@sterlingpublishing.com.

Manufactured in China

Lot #:
2 4 6 8 10 9 7 5 3 1
06/20

sterlingpublishing.com

Cover and interior design by Irene Vandervoort

The NINTH NIGHT of HANUKKAH

by Erica S. Perl

illustrated by Shahar Kober

STERLING CHILDREN'S BOOKS
New York

On the **first night** of Hanukkah, Mom couldn't
find the menorah.
"Special delivery!" said Dad, arriving with pizza.
Max and Rachel looked at each other.
No menorah? No latkes?

"It's just for tonight," said Mom. "I'm sure
we'll find our Hanukkah things tomorrow."
Exhausted from unpacking, the family sat
down to dinner in their new apartment.

It was nice . . . but it didn't
feel quite like Hanukkah.

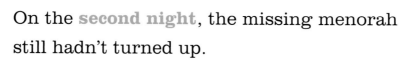

On the **second night**, the missing menorah
still hadn't turned up.
"Should we go to the store?" asked Max.
"No, we'll find it soon," said Rachel. "Besides,
I have an idea for tonight."

Rachel made a beautiful menorah.
Max helped her decorate it.

But when it came time to light the candles,
Mom realized she packed them with the menorah.

"Now should we go to the store?" asked Max.
Mom checked her watch and shook her head.
"Everything's probably closed by now."

Max and Rachel convinced Mom to let them ask
one neighbor.

They knocked on 2C, right next door, and explained
the situation to Mrs. Mendez.

"Would these work?"
she asked.

"Maybe," said Rachel.

Dad lit the *shamash*. Max and Rachel
each used it to light a candle.
Then Max and Rachel both got presents.

It was nice . . . but it didn't
feel quite like Hanukkah.

On the **third night**, Dad offered to make latkes.
He just needed to find his lucky latke pan.
As Dad searched through box after box, Max
followed his nose downstairs . . .

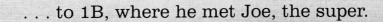
. . . to 1B, where he met Joe, the super.

"Welcome to the building," said Joe. "Need anything? Let me know." "Anything?" asked Max, eyeing the steaming platter. Joe happily shared.

It was nice . . . but it didn't feel quite like Hanukkah.

On the **fourth night**, Max said, "Let's play dreidel!"
One problem: no dreidel.
"I'm beginning to think one of our boxes got lost,"
said Dad.
So, Mom called the moving company.
And Max and Rachel set out to find a dreidel.

The Watson twins, who lived upstairs
in 3B, didn't have one.
But they did have a toy that could
spin and spin.

It was nice . . . but it didn't
feel quite like Hanukkah.

On the **fifth night**, Max and Rachel figured out a way to play dreidel.

Which meant they needed gelt.

"No chocolate coins, but I do have these,"
said Mr. Patel, in 4A.

It was nice . . . but it didn't
feel quite like Hanukkah.

On the **sixth night**, Rachel wanted to have
a Hanukkah sing-along.
But Mom's guitar hadn't arrived yet.
"Gigi has one!" shouted the Watson twins,
running up to 5C.

It turned out they were **almost** right.

Mom taught Gigi the chords to "Rock of Ages," and everyone sang.

It was nice . . . but it didn't feel quite like Hanukkah.

On the **seventh night**, Max and Rachel
discovered they were missing something else.
"How do you wrap a present without wrapping
paper?"
On their way outside, they saw Dr. Lee reading
in the lobby.

When they asked him where to buy wrapping
paper, he handed them the comics.
"Try using these," suggested Dr. Lee.
So, they did.

It was nice . . . but it **still** didn't
feel quite like Hanukkah.

On the **eighth night**, Max realized what their
Hanukkah needed: jelly donuts!
It took knocking on several doors, but finally Max
got his jelly.
From the twins' mom in 3B.

Just not in donut form.

"That was nice . . ." said Rachel, as they walked downstairs.

Max took a big bite and finished her thought:

"*Mmuht it mmuhsn't* feel quite like Hummukkuh."

The next morning, there was a knock at the door.
"Special delivery!"
Only this time, it wasn't Dad or pizza.
And it wasn't the long-lost box.

"Let's have a Hanukkah sing-along tonight," suggested Mom.

"Last night was the eighth night," Rachel reminded her.
"It won't be Hanukkah anymore."

"Maybe it should be,"
said Max, pointing.
"Nine candles, nine
nights."

Rachel's eyes lit up.
She whispered to
Max.

Max whispered back, and together they
developed a plan.

With a box of candles and a box of crayons,
they set it in motion.

That evening, Max and Rachel waited.

And waited.

"Maybe this isn't going to work," said Max.

"It'll work," said Rachel, sounding more confident than she felt.

Just then, there was a knock at the door.

And another. And another.

Max and Rachel thanked them all for coming.

Then they explained the reason for their
Shamash Night celebration.
"For eight nights of Hanukkah, the *shamash*
helps light all the other candles," said Max.
"Like all of you helped us," added Rachel. "So, we
wanted to say thanks—to the *shamash* and to you."
Just then, a voice called out from the back of the
line of guests.

"Special delivery!"

"The missing box!" said Mom.

"Now *that's* what I call a miracle!" said Dad.

In the box, Max and Rachel found
their family menorah,
Hanukkah candles,
Dad's lucky latke pan,
dreidels and gelt,
wrapping paper,
and Aunt Edith's recipe
for jelly donuts.

HANUKKAH
CANDLES

Jelly Donuts

So, on the **ninth night** in their new home,
Max and Rachel and their new friends
talked and laughed,
ate and played games,
sang and danced by the light of many candles.

It was nice.
Really
REALLY
nice.
And best of all,
it felt *exactly*
like Hanukkah.

Author's note

Hanukkah, the festival of lights, commemorates the victory of a small, ragtag band of Maccabean soldiers over the far more powerful Greek/Syrian forces of King Antiochus in the year 165 B.C.E. The legend is that after the Maccabees regained control of the defiled and damaged Temple, there was only enough lamp oil for one night, and yet—miraculously—it burned for eight nights. For this reason, we say blessings and light candles each night of Hanukkah. We start by lighting one candle—using the *shamash*, or helper candle—the first night, and we add one additional candle each night until all the candles are lit on the eighth and final night of the holiday. The word *shamash* is Hebrew and is pronounced "shah-MAHsh." The Yiddish word *shammes*, which is what many families (including my own) use, is pronounced "SHAH-miss."

A Hanukkah tradition in my family is for everyone to choose a candle and root for it to burn the longest. One night, while making their selections, my two daughters wondered out loud why we didn't give the shamash its own night of honor for spending eight nights helping the other candles. The discussion that followed lit the flame of inspiration for *The Ninth Night of Hanukkah*.

Like the *shamash*, individual people have the power to spark change and brighten the lives of those around them. That's why Hanukkah is the perfect time for all of us to show appreciation for those who help us, help others, and help heal the world. And if it means keeping the menorah and the latke pan out for one more night to do so—well, who can argue with that?

I wish you and yours a happy Hanukkah and a joyous "Shamash Night."

—Erica

How to Create Your Own "Shamash Night"

Here are some ideas from me and my congregation,
Temple Micah, in Washington, DC.

1. Gather family, friends, and/or community members.

2. Read *The Ninth Night of Hanukkah* aloud and discuss it.
   Why do Max and Rachel want to thank their neighbors? Why do they tape a candle to each invitation? What makes their celebration feel "just like Hanukkah" even though the eighth night has passed?

3. Celebrate helping! Share songs, dances, games, crafts, and skills someone helped you learn. (For example, my mom helped me learn how to knit.) Enjoy foods someone helped you make or taught you how to make—and share that person's name and recipe.

4. Celebrate helpers! Invite everyone to brainstorm a list of helpers in their day-to-day life—this can include neighbors (like in the book), but also librarians, teachers, babysitters, dog walkers, crossing guards, postal workers, trash collectors, and newspaper deliverers.

5. Write each helper's name—and/or way of helping—on a single, candle-shaped strip of construction paper. You can display these on a backdrop. Or, using tape or a stapler, you can make them into linked rings and create an impressive chain of helpers.

6. Make a thank-you note for each helper. Be creative—thanks can be expressed with words and art in so many ways!

7. Tape a Hanukkah candle to each note and explain its significance. For example, you can write: *During Hanukkah, the shamash candle gives light to all the other candles. We are thankful to you because, like the shamash candle, your light helps to brighten our days.*

8. Mail or hand-deliver these special notes of appreciation—on their own or with anything else you wish to add (high-fives, hugs, and baked goods are nice ideas).

9. Pass it on! Share images and stories from your #ShamashNight. You might inspire others to join you and start their own Shamash Night traditions!